# FUNNY MAN

by Margo Sorenson

Cover and Inside Illustrations: Sue Cornelison

To my wonderful family, Jim, Jill, Jane, and Chris, for their loving support and for putting up with this kind of humor for so long
To Bonnie and Vicky for encouraging me to continue, despite gators in the swamps
To KT and Michael for their ideas and insights

## About the Author

Margo Sorenson was born in Washington, D.C. She spent the first seven years of her life in Europe, living where there were few children her age. She found books to be her best friends and read constantly. Ms. Sorenson wrote her own stories too.

Ms. Sorenson finished her school years in California, graduating from the University of California at Los Angeles. She taught high school and middle school and raised a family of two daughters. Ms. Sorenson is now a full-time writer, writing primarily for young people.

After having lived in Hawaii and California, Ms. Sorenson now splits her time living in California and Minnesota with her husband. She enjoys traveling to Europe and visiting places she might write about. When she isn't writing, she enjoys reading, sports, and traveling.

Printed in the United States of America. For information, contact
Perfection Learning® Corporation
1000 North Second Avenue, P.O. Box 500
Logan, Iowa 51546-0500.
Phone: 1-800-831-4190
Fax: 1-800-543-2745
perfectionlearning.com
RLB ISBN-13: 978-0-7569-0899-7
RLB ISBN-10: 0-7569-0899-x
PB ISBN-13: 978-0-7891-5733-1
PB ISBN-10: 0-7891-5733-0
4 5 6 7 8 9 PP 13 12 11 10 09 08
Printed in the U.S.A.

# Contents

# CHapter one

# No JoKe

"Hey, Derrick! Hey, Funny Man!"

Derrick stopped in front of his locker and turned around. He grinned at his friends, Rod and Shaun.

"What's up?" he asked, pulling out his English book.

"Yeah, like you don't know, Funny Man," Shaun joked. "I can't believe what you did in science!"

Derrick smiled and shrugged his shoulders.

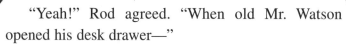

"Yeah!" Rod agreed. "When old Mr. Watson opened his desk drawer—"

"And he held up the rubber frog—" Shaun broke in.

"With the sign you taped on it," Rod continued. "*Hop to it!* Just like he always yells at us in class—"

"I thought I was gonna fall out of my chair laughing!" Shaun finished. He and Rod bumped fists.

Derrick laughed. "Yeah. I had Jermaine print the sign. Otherwise, Mr. Watson would know it was me."

"Uh-huh," Shaun snorted. "Because it usually *is*!" They began walking down the crowded hall.

"How do you always think of that stuff?" Rod asked admiringly.

Derrick shook his head. "I don't know," he said. "I just do."

"Being in classes with you is almost better than watching Eddie Murphy or Chris Rock," Shaun said. *"Almost."*

"Thanks," Derrick said. Then he sighed. "Too bad I can't get good grades for my jokes." He frowned. "I could be out of football before the end of the season. Dowling the Dragon is giving me a D in English."

He stopped in front of the door to their English class. The boys halted.

"The Dragon is after me all the time," Derrick complained.

"Yeah," Rod agreed. "*She* doesn't think you're too funny!" He snickered.

"Wonder why?" Shaun said, smirking.

Derrick grinned. "She wasn't too crazy about the dragon poem I wrote. The one with the bad breath flames. Think she guessed it was about her?"

The boys laughed. Rod clapped him on the back.

Then Derrick shrugged. "You can't make everybody happy, I guess."

Rod and Shaun hooted as Derrick led the way into class. Dowling the Dragon glared at him over the top of her glasses. He sighed and dropped down into his desk.

"Let's have it quiet, class," Mrs. Dowling snapped. She frowned at Derrick. "Take out your notebooks."

"She's already burping fire," Derrick whispered to Rod next to him.

"Mmmmph!" Rod choked out, trying to keep from laughing. His shoulders shook, and he buried his head on his desk.

"Is there a problem, Derrick?" Mrs. Dowling's voice sent chills down his spine.

"No, ma'am," Derrick said. He opened his eyes wide. "Rod was just looking for a Kleenex. He has a cold."

All around him, he could hear other students beginning to chuckle and snort.

"Well, you just come on up and get one for him," Mrs. Dowling said. Her eyes narrowed at Derrick. "How nice that you're so concerned about your fellow students."

Derrick slid out of his desk. He walked up to the front of the room. Mrs. Dowling held out a Kleenex.

"Derrick," Mrs. Dowling said in a low voice.

Her blue eyes bore into his. Derrick tried not to flinch. Her breath could kill a horse.

"Your midterm grade was a D," she continued. "It's nice that you can keep everyone in class laughing. But you need to pay attention."

"Uh-huh," Derrick muttered. He could almost see her breathing smoke through her nostrils. He bit his tongue to keep from busting up.

Dowling the Dragon stepped closer to him. "I know you want to play football. But with a D in English, your touchdown days are going to be over."

Derrick winced. She was right. If he wanted to play football, he needed at least a C-. The school was tough on eligibility. Coach Harris had been after him for weeks. His parents were on his case too.

"So?" Dowling the Dragon peered at him. "Derrick?"

"Um, yes, ma'am," Derrick mumbled. "I'll do better."

"Use your talent," Mrs. Dowling urged him. Then she sighed. "You could do so well."

"Uh-huh," Derrick said. He began walking back to his seat. He glanced quickly over his shoulder. Mrs. Dowling was writing something on the whiteboard.

Everyone was watching him. He grinned. Suddenly, he stuck his hands out in front of him as if they were dragon claws. He stomped down the aisle like Godzilla. Giggles and laughter spread through the room.

"Derrick!" Mrs. Dowling's voice ripped through the air.

But Derrick had already dropped into the safety of his seat, not a second too soon. He smiled innocently at Mrs. Dowling.

She folded her arms. "Start taking notes, class," she warned. "This is your grammar homework."

Derrick glanced at Shaun and Rod. They grinned at him. As long as he could keep everyone laughing, he could stand English class. Then his grin faded. He still had to do something about his English grade and football.

After school, Derrick sat with his teammates on a bench by the football field. Coach Harris paced up and down.

"We have a good start to the season," Coach was saying. He pounded his fist into his open hand. "With Shaun as quarterback and Derrick as wide receiver, we've done well."

Derrick flushed with pride. He sat up straighter.

"But midterms were last week." Coach Harris frowned. "Quarter grades are coming out in four weeks. Some of you have eligibility problems."

Derrick wanted to shrink on the bench. Shaun elbowed him.

"You know who you are," Coach said. "Let's focus."

"Focus? But I'm not a camera," Derrick joked.

A few snickers broke out along the bench. The coach's face began to turn purple. Silence fell over the team. Derrick wanted to kick himself.

"Farley, I'll see you after practice—*again*," Coach growled. "And you'll do four laps first. All right, team. Let's get going."

"Whooooeeee," Shaun whispered to Derrick. "You got Coach mad again, bro." They jogged to the middle of the field. "That *was* funny though."

Derrick grimaced. "I don't think Coach thought it was too funny." Derrick dropped to the grass and stretched. "He's been all over me about my attitude."

"Yeah," Shaun said. He sat down on the ground, reaching for his shoe.

"You know," Derrick went on. "Get serious about practice, blah, blah, blah." Derrick shook his head. He turned to look at Shaun. "I mean, why can't people take a joke?"

Shaun grinned. "I don't know. All I know is if they're around you, they'd better learn how!"

Derrick laughed.

"Farley and Endicott!" Coach's voice barked across the field. "Get moving!"

"Get moving!" Derrick muttered under his breath. "I'm not a van."

Shaun laughed.

After practice, Derrick ran his laps. In the locker room, he grabbed his backpack from his locker. Coach Harris walked into the locker room.

"Good luck," Shaun whispered to Derrick.

"Farley, in my office," Coach Harris ordered.

Derrick held back a sigh. "Yes, Coach," he answered. He trudged between the long benches. Derrick could hear guys quietly saying "good luck" and "hang tough."

Coach shut the door behind Derrick. Hands on his hips, he stared at Derrick.

"For someone with a lot of talent, you sure have a big mouth," Coach said.

Derrick swallowed hard.

"Yes, sir," he mumbled.

"I mean, really, Farley," Coach went on. "You could help take our middle school team all the way to the league championship. But I can't have someone mouthing off." Coach sighed and folded his arms. "Practice is serious. We have to concentrate. I can't have my players cracking up all the time over some dumb comment you've made."

"No, sir," Derrick said. He stared at the floor.

"Discipline is key in this game," Coach said. "You have to show some discipline. Exercise some self-restraint. Or," he said, grabbing a clipboard off the desk, "you're benched."

Derrick's mouth felt dry.

"Benched?" he squeaked. "But, Coach—"

"Control yourself, Farley," Coach snapped. "Pay attention in practice. And then there's your English grade." He tapped the clipboard. Derrick saw his grade sheet clipped to the top.

Derrick's heart sank.

"I've been talking to Mrs. Dowling," Coach went on. "You have the same problem in English as on the football field. And you're not doing the work you should. More wasted talent, Farley," he finished.

He slapped the clipboard down. "Now get home. Do your homework. And keep that mouth shut in practice," he warned. "You're lucky I didn't make you do *more* laps."

"Yes, Coach," Derrick groaned. His shoulders drooped. Everyone was after him now.

When the city bus pulled up at his stop, Derrick jumped down the steps. At least Mom and Dad wouldn't be home from work. He didn't need another lecture from them right now.

But Craig would be home. Derrick sighed. What had he done to deserve an older brother like Craig?

Derrick walked in the front door. Of course, Mr. Do-Everything-Right Craig was probably already doing his homework.

"That you?" Craig's voice echoed from the kitchen.

"Well, it isn't Michael Jordan," Derrick called. He dumped his backpack on the floor.

"Ha, ha," Craig answered. "Funny man."

Derrick walked into the kitchen and opened the refrigerator. He peered at the cans and bottles.

"Why are you late?" Craig asked. "Get in trouble again?"

"Nah," Derrick said. Not really, he told himself. "Coach wanted to talk to me."

Craig looked up from his books. "Open your mouth in practice again?" he asked.

"Not exactly," Derrick fibbed. He gurgled a can of pop noisily.

"Figures. For a kid as smart as you, you sure can get yourself into trouble," Craig said. He leaned back in his chair. "When are you going to grow up?"

"I *am* grown-up," Derrick protested. "I'm just not a snotty, know-it-all, big-time senior like you."

"You wish," Craig snapped. "*You'll* be lucky to make it to your senior year. Especially with your English grade." A sly grin crept across his face. "And you may not be playing football either. Mom and Dad aren't too happy. You'd better get your act together."

"*You* stay out of my business," Derrick warned. "Don't you have some more of your A+ work to do?"

Craig shook his head. "As if you'd even know A+ work if you ever saw it." He smirked. "Mom and Dad are tired of hassling with you, you know. It's tough for them at work right now. They think you should get a job to help out, remember?"

Derrick winced. He tried not to think about that. They'd talked to him just last week about a job.

Craig went on. "And you just keep messing around. Don't you think you could try to act your age?"

"Yeah, yeah, yeah," Derrick said. "Look in the dictionary under *mature* and there's a picture of you, right?" he snorted.

Craig's face darkened. But he just picked up his pen and began writing.

Derrick gulped down the rest of the can. He tossed it into the recycling bin.

Fine, he told himself. Just fine. First it was Dowling the Dragon and the bad English grade. Then it was Coach Harris and being serious in practice. Next it would be his parents and getting a job.

It looked as if no one wanted a funny man.

# cHapter tWo

# THe FUN IS Over

An hour later, Derrick clicked off the TV. There was nothing else new on the comedy channel. He'd already seen the Bernie Mac and D. L. Hughley special. He punched a pillow on the couch.

Mom and Dad would be pulling up in the driveway any minute. He'd better look as if he were doing his homework.

He stared at his papers and books lying on the floor. Maybe Craig thought he'd been studying while he watched TV. Then Craig wouldn't get him in more trouble with his parents.

Derrick almost snorted. Yeah, right. Living with Craig was like living with the secret police in Russia. He was always lecturing Derrick. That was almost worse than having Mom and Dad on his case.

Derrick slumped back on the couch. Craig was smart. He worked hard at his job. And he ran track too. He did everything right. Derrick made a face.

"We're home!" Mom's voice called from the back door.

Before he could slide over next to his books, Dad walked into the living room. His eyebrows slanted angrily.

"Watching TV again? No homework, eh? Nothing better to do?" he asked. "Your mom and I are tired from working all day long. And you just sit on the couch and watch your comedians." He shook his head.

Derrick's face got hot.

"Uh, really, Dad," he stammered. "I was just—"

Mom walked in. Derrick stopped.

She looked at the books and papers on the floor. "Oh, Derrick," she sighed. "Just once it would be so nice to come home from work and see you actually *doing* homework." Her shoulders seemed to droop right in front of him. Dad glanced at her worriedly. Then he looked back at Derrick.

Derrick cracked his knuckles. Here came another lecture from Dad.

"Your grades are lousy," Dad began. He shook his finger at Derrick. "You might get kicked out of football. And look at your mom." He gestured to Mom. "She's beat. And why? She's working too hard. And today the warehouse told us they can't give us a raise this year."

Uh-oh, Derrick thought. More money problems.

Dad walked closer. "We talked to you last week about getting a job. You're going to need new football shoes. And we're tired of paying for your videos and your fun. It's time for you to pull your own weight." He picked up the remote and shook it in the air. "No more funny-man stuff, you hear?"

Derrick bit back what he wanted to say. *How about funny-guy stuff?* Somehow, he knew Dad wouldn't like that one.

"Craig said that Joe, his boss at Taste of Italy, needs a busboy," Mom said. She brushed her hair back from her face. Wearily, she dropped down on the couch.

Derrick's heart sank. "Aw, Mom!" he complained. "I don't wanna work at the same place as Craig!" That would be the worst, he told himself.

"Look here, Derrick," Dad barked. "You may not have a choice. No one else will hire a 14-year-old." He stared at Derrick. "And don't forget your reputation around the neighborhood as Mr. Comedian." Dad sighed. "You'd have a tough time getting a job. At least Joe might hire you because of Craig. He depends on Craig. Craig is a hard worker."

Derrick took a deep breath. There it was again. Craig was Mr. Perfect. It was enough to make him barf.

Craig walked in from the kitchen. "Somebody talking about me?" he asked. He carried a book under his arm.

Derrick wanted to punch his smug face. "Yeah, we're singing your praises again," he snapped. "Sorry. No new verses. Just the same old ones."

Dad's face darkened. He shook his finger at Derrick again. "You listen up," he growled. "You have a lot to learn. You need to start showing your mother and me some responsibility by getting a job. Otherwise, we'll start cutting out your fun. And that means no football too. *If* you're still eligible, that is," he added.

*And when will I be eligible for a break?* Derrick wanted to ask. But he bit back the words.

From the corner of his eye, Derrick saw Craig hide a smile. That jerk! Derrick clenched his fists.

"You'd better talk to Joe," Mom told Derrick.

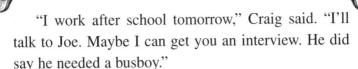 

"I work after school tomorrow," Craig said. "I'll talk to Joe. Maybe I can get you an interview. He did say he needed a busboy."

"That's nice, Craig," Mom said.

Derrick swallowed his words. *That's sooooooo sweet, Craigie*, he wanted to spit out.

"But you'd better be the man," Craig warned. He shook his book at Derrick. "I don't want to lose my job because of you, meathead. The Taste of Italy isn't Comedy Central or *Saturday Night at the Apollo*."

"Listen to your brother," Dad said. "This is a chance for you to prove you're growing up."

"You'll be in high school next year," Mom reminded him.

"If he passes English," Craig joked. He laughed at his own joke. Lame, Derrick thought. No one laughs at his own jokes.

"Craig!" Mom said. "Enough is enough."

Derrick gave Craig a hard look. He wouldn't *fail* English. But would his grade be high enough to stay in football?

"Sorry, Mom," Craig said quickly.

What a kiss-up, Derrick thought. If only Shaun and Rod could hear Craig. They'd fall over laughing.

"I'll set Derrick up for Friday after the football game," Craig promised. He stared at Derrick. "Remember what I said," he threatened. "I need to keep this job."

"Yeah, yeah, yeah," Derrick mumbled. Great—now he had to go to a job interview on Friday after the game. That meant no hanging with his buddies. No watching Steve Harvey's *Best of the Apollo* reruns. No *Austin Powers* or *Dumb and Dumber* for the hundredth time. No old Chevy Chase movies. No Wayans brothers shows. What was a Friday night without comedy?

Derrick glanced at Craig. Would Joe give him a job just because of Craig? Then his stomach tightened. What if Joe knew too much about what a goof-off Derrick was? What if he didn't get the job?

If Joe didn't want him, then what? Dad had said no football. Shaun and Rod would be playing without him. Derrick sighed. He'd better get the job.

"And bring up that English grade," Dad reminded.

Mom sat up. "You're smart enough, Derrick."

"Hmph," Dad snorted. "Keep a rein on that mouth. Your English grade isn't too funny, bud."

*Maybe not, but you should see my English teacher*, Derrick wanted to say. But he clamped his mouth shut.

"Set the table, please, Derrick," Mom said. She pulled herself up off the couch and walked to the kitchen.

After dinner, Derrick sat in the bedroom he shared with Craig. His backpack lay on the bed next to him. He'd brought the *TV Guide* in to check out the upcoming comedy shows. He found an article on the old movie series, *Beverly Hills Cop*.

Derrick flipped through the article. Those guys got paid for being funny. All *he* got was trouble. He tossed the magazine aside and opened his English book. Life was closing in on him. He was doomed.

Two days passed in a blur of homework and school. During Friday afternoon's football game, Derrick sat on the bench for the first half.

"Coach *said* he'd bench me," he grumbled to Rod. "But I didn't think he'd do it this soon."

"I sit on the bench all the time." Rod shrugged. "But then I don't have your speed." He rested his chin on his hands. "Wish I did. I'd rather be benched for a smart-mouth attitude than for just being too slow."

"Huh," Derrick grunted.

"Farley!" Coach Harris called out after halftime. "You're in."

Derrick shot up off the bench. As he ran by, Coach grabbed his arm.

"You've paid for that attitude—for now," Coach said. "Just watch it. We need you on the field. Now get out there and score!"

"Okay, Coach," Derrick said. He jogged to his position. Maybe Coach would keep him on the team, even if he did get a D in English.

Derrick looked over at his coach. He stood on the sidelines, staring intently at the field. Derrick's stomach did a small flip. No way. Coach never cut anyone any slack. He had to get his grade up.

Derrick caught the winning touchdown pass just before the whistle blew. In the locker room, everyone was hooting and howling like they always did after a win.

"Hey, Derrick! Good run," Shaun said. He snapped a towel at Derrick.

Derrick grinned. "Nice pass," he answered. Then he flexed his muscles. "Of course, it took real talent to snag it."

"Yeah, right!" Shaun said. "Wanna come over for dinner? I don't know what my grandma is cooking."

Derrick almost said yeah. Then he remembered and sighed.

"Nah. I can't." He sank down on the bench. "I have to go by Taste of Italy," he said.

"You have to do something for Craig?" Shaun asked. "Get out of it!"

Derrick shook his head glumly. "It's worse than that. I have a job interview, remember?"

"Oh, yeah," Shaun said. He pulled on his sneakers. "You have to be all grown-up now, right?"

"Uh-huh," Derrick grumbled. "I'd better draw wrinkles on my face or something. Maybe wear a tie to school." He shrugged. "My parents are all over me. English grade. Football. Attitude." He laced up his shoes partway, leaving the laces untied at the top. He stood up. "They just don't get it," he complained.

"Yeah," Shaun said. "Too bad."

"What's too bad is I have to get this job," Derrick said. "I'm dust if I don't. And if I *do*, I won't have a life."

"Good luck," Shaun said. He bumped fists with Derrick. "See ya, bro."

"Yeah," Derrick sighed. "See ya."

As he left the school grounds, his mouth felt dry. It was only three blocks to Taste of Italy. And then what?

Would Joe give him a bad time about stuff? Lots of people in the neighborhood must have told Joe stories. Derrick cringed a little.

Had Joe heard about the stuff he always said in school? What about last Halloween when he decorated the neighbors' trees with toilet paper? Or the water-balloon blast this summer in front of the Greek grocery? No one got hurt, he could argue. And lots of people thought he was funny.

But not his parents.

Not his teachers.

Not Coach Harris.

And maybe not Joe.

And if Joe didn't give him a job, then there'd be no football. And if he couldn't play football, he had no life.

Derrick stopped. The red and green sign above the restaurant read "Taste of Italy." He took a deep breath and opened the door.

# cHapter tHree

# SicK!

Shoving his hands in his pockets, Derrick walked inside. He smelled garlic. Some people sat eating at tables with red-and-white checked tablecloths.

Craig carried in a platter of spaghetti. Had Craig said anything good about him to Joe? He'd better have. Craig began to set the platter down carefully in front of a customer.

Derrick grinned. What if he yelled, "Look out!" Craig would jump. Maybe he'd even drop the spaghetti in the guy's lap! Derrick shook his head. Not a good idea, he thought.

Derrick spotted Joe. Wearing a red-and-white apron, he was talking to some people at a table. Derrick's stomach tightened.

Joe picked up the menus. He turned around. Seeing Derrick, Joe walked over quickly. Derrick swallowed hard.

"Derrick," Joe said. He wiped his hands on his apron. Then he held out a hand.

Derrick shook it. "Uh-huh," he said.

Joe looked at him. "You *are* young." He frowned. "Your grades all right in school?" he asked.

Derrick's face turned warm. "Uh, yeah. They're okay," he fibbed.

"Good," Joe said. "You don't mind hard work?"

Derrick tried not to look down at the floor. "Uh-uh," he answered. He stopped the words that wanted to spill out. *But hard work minds me!* No smart mouth now, he warned himself.

"Hmmm," Joe said. He sighed. "You're definitely young," he repeated. "But because of Craig, I'll give you a chance," he said. "I need a busboy now."

Thwack! He slapped the menus on his open hand. Derrick jumped a little.

"But you have to work hard," Joe told him. "Since we've moved to this new, larger location, we need to attract new customers. And we have to keep the old ones."

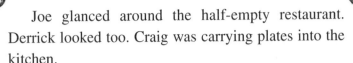 

Joe glanced around the half-empty restaurant. Derrick looked too. Craig was carrying plates into the kitchen.

Joe went on. "A bigger place means bigger bills." A frown crossed his face. He slapped the menus again. "If business doesn't grow, I'll have to let you go."

"Okay," Derrick said. Then he'd be free again! He hesitated. Nope. No way. Mom and Dad would just make him look for another job. Or they'd make him quit football.

"All right," Joe said abruptly. "Can you work a couple of hours on Tuesdays and Thursdays at dinnertime? And all day Saturdays?"

"Uh, um, uh, sure!" Derrick blurted. "I have football practice during the week. But I can be here at 5:00. Is that okay?"

Joe nodded. "You'll stay till 7:00."

He had the job! That wasn't too hard, Derrick thought.

Joe looked intently at Derrick. "I'm counting on you," he warned. "Come tomorrow afternoon at 2:30. There'll be time to train you before the dinner rush—if we even *have* a dinner rush."

"Thanks, Joe," Derrick said. "See you tomorrow."

"Be on time," Joe added. Then he vanished into the kitchen.

Craig walked over to Derrick. Derrick gave Craig a half-salute. "Thanks, bro," he said.

Craig stared at Derrick. "Just don't screw up," he said. Then he turned on his heel. The kitchen doors whooshed behind him.

*Jerk!* Derrick wanted to yell back at him. But customers were watching. He'd get fired before he even started.

Derrick left and walked home. He kicked some cans on the sidewalk. Right! he snapped silently. Don't screw up! What about having fun in life?

"Good, Derrick," Mom said later that night when Derrick told his parents he got the job. "You're on your way."

"You'd better not mess up, meathead," Craig said. "Don't make me look bad." He frowned at Derrick.

*You're the meathead serving meatballs,* Derrick wanted to say.

But just then, Dad spoke up. "It's time to prove yourself," he said. "Your English grade too. Bring it up."

"Yeah, bring it up, right," Derrick blustered. "I'll bring something up—English." He stuck his finger down his throat. "Aaaaaakkkk," he gagged.

"Derrick!" Mom complained. Craig rolled his eyes.

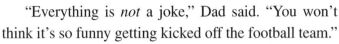
"Everything is *not* a joke," Dad said. "You won't think it's so funny getting kicked off the football team."

Derrick walked to his room in silence. He could do the restaurant job—no problem. Now his English grade—*that* was another story.

Late Saturday afternoon, Derrick felt sweat running down his face. Joe had shown him how to bus tables. "Be efficient," he'd ordered. But Joe had cracked a few jokes during the training. He wasn't such a bad guy, Derrick decided.

Now Derrick was getting ready for the dinner hour. Garlic and sausage smells drifted through the restaurant.

Grabbing a clean cloth and spray cleaner, Derrick wiped tables. Then he began to set them. In the kitchen, Craig chopped vegetables. Joe worked on sauces.

The fan was running overhead. But heat from the kitchen drifted into the dining room.

"Can't run the air conditioner," Joe said, when Derrick walked in the kitchen to complain. Joe mopped his face. "Gotta save money. It'll cool down later." He kept stirring a huge pot of simmering red sauce. With a sigh, Derrick walked back into the dining room.

"Yo! Derrick!" Familiar voices called to Derrick. He looked up and stopped rolling silverware in napkins.

A grin spread across his face. "Hey! Shaun! Rod!" he answered. He was glad to see his buddies. He needed a break.

"What's up?" Shaun asked. The two boys walked over. They all bumped fists.

"Aw, just working," Derrick said. He gestured to the empty tables. "Getting ready."

"Ready for what?" Rod asked, looking around. "There's no one here."

"People will come," Derrick said. "At least, we *hope* they will."

"You don't look like you're working too hard," Shaun joked.

"Oh, no?" Derrick asked. He unfolded a napkin and plopped it on his head.

"Allow me!" he teased, bowing low and sweeping his arm through the air. "Your table, sirs!"

Shaun and Rod busted up laughing. Derrick joined in their laughter.

The doors to the kitchen swung open.

"What's going on in here?" Joe barked. Under his chef's hat, his red face matched his apron. He put his hands on his hips.

Derrick flinched. Uh-oh. He was dust now. He whipped the napkin off his head.

"Ah, nothing," he said quickly.

"I don't know who you guys are," Joe said, "but you're bothering my busboy. Now get out."

"Sorry!" Rod squeaked. Shaun and Rod hustled out the door.

"And you . . ." Joe began. "What do you think you're doing? This is a place of business, not a comedy act."

"I—I'm sorry," Derrick mumbled. He grabbed some silverware.

"What happened?" Craig asked from the doorway.

"Uh—nothing," Derrick stammered. "Just—ah—some of my buddies came in."

Joe frowned at Derrick. "This better not happen again," he warned.

"Uh, sure, no problem," Derrick promised. "Sorry!"

Craig shook his head and disappeared into the kitchen.

"I have bills to pay," Joe reminded him. "I need your help, not your jokes, to keep customers."

"Uh, sure," Derrick said. Joe walked back into the kitchen.

Derrick's face felt warm. He felt kind of bad. But the restaurant being empty wasn't his problem, was it? He began rolling up silverware again.

Then Derrick shook his head. But it *was* his problem, he admitted. If there wasn't enough business, he wouldn't have a job. Derrick's shoulders slumped. He kept rolling silverware, glancing up at the door. Where were all the customers?

Derrick was almost happy when Monday arrived. At least his nagging parents couldn't follow him to school. All weekend, they'd been hassling him.

It was like a boring song playing over and over again. Derrick almost told Mom and Dad the rap verses he'd made up. *If you can't get a job, you are just a slob. If you can't pass your English, you're gonna be finished.* He half-smiled. That would have really pushed them over the edge though. So he'd kept quiet.

"All right, class," Mrs. Dowling called out at the beginning of class. "Get out your notebooks. I have the topic of your next paper assignment for you."

"How to raise baby dragons," Derrick whispered to Shaun.

Shaun couldn't hold back his laughter. Around the class, kids started to laugh too.

Dowling the Dragon stopped. She stared at Derrick. "I have no idea what's so funny about a paper," she said. "Please pay attention."

Derrick stifled a groan.

"Now," Mrs. Dowling went on, "you're going to write an essay. It will be your opinion of some part of the health-care system. Doctors, hospitals, high costs, patient privacy—anything in the health industry."

"*Health* care?" Derrick blurted out. *"Sick!"* he joked.

Everyone began hooting and howling.

"Fine, Derrick," Dowling the Dragon snarled. "Perhaps detention will make you more serious."

"Uh, no, ma'am," Derrick said quickly. "Sorry. It just popped out."

Mrs. Dowling sighed. She tapped the dry-erase marker on the whiteboard. "I'll be giving each of you some articles to read about health care. Then you form your viewpoint with facts to support your opinion."

Facts, Derrick sighed. Support. This wasn't going to be easy. Of course, English never was.

Dowling the Dragon was still blabbing. "Write with a strong sense of personal voice. Write it like a letter to the editor of the newspaper."

Ugh, thought Derrick. Write with a personal voice. That meant write it as if he really cared. What if he didn't care?

Mrs. Dowling stared right at Derrick. Could she read his mind? he wondered.

"This paper will be worth 25 percent of your quarter grade," she warned. "For some of you . . ."

She paused. She was still looking at Derrick. He shrank down in his chair.

" . . . this could make the difference in your grade," she finished. "It could mean passing with a C- or not!"

Great, Derrick told himself. Grabbing a pencil, he copied down the dates she wrote on the board.

After class, Mrs. Dowling stepped in front of him. "Derrick," she said. Her gaze locked with his. "You need at least a B on this essay. Otherwise you'll get a D in English."

"But football!" Derrick exclaimed.

"I know, Derrick," Mrs. Dowling said firmly. "That's why I wanted to give you this extra warning."

"Uh, thanks," Derrick muttered.

"You have a lot of ability," she said. She shook her head. "Find a way to use it for English."

"Yeah," Derrick said. He shouldered his backpack. "Uh, see ya," he said.

Later, at the end of football practice, Coach Harris called everyone in off the field. The team dropped to the grass. Derrick wiped his sweaty forehead with his shirtsleeve.

"Not a bad practice," Coach began.

"Not a good one either," Derrick blurted out.

Some guys grinned. A couple of them laughed. Rod elbowed him.

"Tell you what, Farley," Coach Harris retorted. "If you were as quick with your feet as you are with your mouth, we wouldn't have that problem."

Derrick felt the blood rush to his forehead. Couldn't anyone give him a break? He really *was* beginning to feel sick.

# CHAPTER FOUR

# NO MORE FUNNY BUSINESS

At home, Derrick flung his backpack on the couch. Craig was at work. Mom and Dad wouldn't be home till dinnertime. Hah! He had the house to himself.

He glanced at his backpack. The English assignment was inside. Dowling the Dragon had passed out the health-care articles in class. He'd begun reading one of them. Health insurance made doctors overworked, the article had said.

Right, Derrick snorted to himself. Doctors were overworked. *He* was overworked. *They* were *overpaid*, he thought.

He looked around the living room at the couch and chairs. All of their stuff was old. They'd gotten some of it at the secondhand store. He bet there weren't any doctors shopping at secondhand stores.

He made a face. That health-care essay was going to be a pain.

"Hah! Health care—a pain!" He snickered. As long as he was alone, he could laugh at his own joke, right?

Then he sighed. Maybe he should work on the essay. He could at least read some more articles. But Dowling the Dragon had given them grammar homework too. That was due Thursday. The essay wasn't due for ten days.

The TV blinked its green clock lights. Wait! It was time for *Top Ten Comedians*. Derrick reached for the remote. He settled back on the couch. English could wait.

Tuesday and Wednesday passed in a blur. No life, Derrick told himself in English class Thursday afternoon. He stared at his grammar book in a daze. He had no life.

He had no time to hang with Shaun and Rod, except at school or practice. He had to scramble to get his homework done. Some of it still wasn't finished.

He'd missed some great comedy specials on HBO too. Worse, Craig forgot to tape them for him. Or at least, that's what he'd *said*, Derrick sneered to himself. Having Craig around was like having a miniature parent on his case all the time.

*Grow up. Do your homework. Don't watch TV.* Craig preached at him all the time.

"Derrick? Are you with us?" Mrs. Dowling's voice cut through the air.

Derrick snapped to attention. "Uh, yes, Mrs. Dowling," he stammered.

"I just asked you to read your answer for number 20 in the grammar exercise," Mrs. Dowling said.

Derrick looked down at his grammar book. Then he covered the sheet of notebook paper on his desk with his hand. Of course, he hadn't done the grammar homework from three days ago.

"Uh, the verb is *watching*, Mrs. Dowling," Derrick answered.

"*Were* watching, Derrick," Mrs. Dowling corrected. "Remember the helping verb."

"Well, it didn't help me," Derrick said. He turned and grinned at Shaun.

The class laughed.

"You might find humor in grammar, Derrick," Dowling the Dragon scolded. "But I assure you, it doesn't find *you* the least bit funny."

Derrick drummed his fingers on the desk. "Sorry," he said.

How could he get her to quit hassling him? he wondered. Maybe he could plug her dragon nostrils, and she'd send smoke out her ears. He hid a grin.

"Pass your papers in, class. And take out your articles for the health-care essay. You need to start working on your outlines. For the rest of today and this week, we'll go to the computer writing lab. You'll do your rough drafts on the computers."

Ugh, Derrick thought. Now he'd *have* to start on his paper.

The students began shuffling papers. Backpacks unzipped and binders snapped open. Derrick flipped through the loose papers in his backpack. Where were those articles? There! Right next to the unfinished science-lab project papers. He grimaced. He wasn't "hopping to it" for Mr. Watson either.

"First I'll be around to see how each of you is doing," Mrs. Dowling announced. "Then we're off to the lab."

Great, Derrick moaned to himself. He'd have to fake having read all the articles. How could he even begin an outline?

He pulled out a fresh sheet of notebook paper. He wrote *Outline* at the top. There, he told himself. That was a start.

He paged through the articles. He picked out one— "Health Care Industry Doesn't Trust Patients." He began to scan the article. Glancing up, he saw Mrs. Dowling start down his aisle.

"Here comes old Dragon Breath," he whispered to Shaun. "Look out! She's flammable! Grab the fire extinguisher!"

Shaun exploded in laughter. Giggles echoed in the room.

"Hmmmm." Mrs. Dowling's voice grated in his ear. "You must be writing something really clever, Derrick. Shaun certainly enjoyed it."

"Uh, no, ma'am," Derrick said. "I just read something about patients. I told Shaun I didn't have much patience with it. Patients—patience? Get it?" he asked hopefully.

Mrs. Dowling just shook her head. Her lips pressed together in a thin line. "Get to work, Derrick," she almost hissed. She peered over his shoulder. "Hmmmm. *Outline*, eh? That's it?" she snorted. "Nice job so far. Maybe some time in detention will help."

Derrick gulped. "Uh, no, please, Mrs. Dowling," he pleaded. "I have to work after practice this afternoon."

Mrs. Dowling sighed. "All right, Derrick. I suppose any activity that keeps you out of trouble is good." She leaned closer to him.

Yuck, dragon breath, Derrick thought. He tried to breathe through his mouth.

"You have a lot of potential, Derrick. Use it." She tapped a pointed nail on his desk.

Derrick stared at her finger. Dragon claw! He stifled a snicker.

"You need to do well on this essay. Don't forget about football," she warned, bending even closer.

"Uh-huh, Mrs. Dowling." Derrick tried not to gasp. The fumes! The fumes! Couldn't she leave? Or at least move away from him? Finally, she turned and walked to the next desk. Derrick slumped in relief.

"Whew," Shaun said in low voice. "You're in deep trouble." He frowned. "And so is the team, if you can't play."

"Uh-huh," Derrick said. He made a face.

"But maybe someone else, like Ricardo, can take your position," Shaun teased. "He's not too bad. He could take over for you."

Derrick tightened his mouth. "I'll do the essay," he vowed. "Don't worry."

Mrs. Dowling finished going around the class. "Pack everything up, class," she commanded. "Let's go to the lab."

Desks and chairs scraped on the floor. Students began talking and laughing. Derrick caught up with Shaun on his way out the door. When they reached the lab, they found stations next to each other.

Derrick flicked on the computer. He grabbed the mouse. Then he stared at the screen.

*Microsoft Word*, the banner read. Great, he sneered silently. Maybe the computer could lend him a word or two. He sure didn't have any.

All around him, he heard the clicking of keyboards as students began to work. He pulled out the articles from his backpack. He looked at his pretend outline.

What now? he asked silently, shuffling the papers back and forth. He had to write something about this sick health-care stuff. And it had to be good or his football career was over.

Derrick slumped down in his chair. In boredom, he tapped a few keys over and over. Anything to fill up the screen so it looked as if he were writing.

The hands on the wall clock crawled around the dial. Dowling the Dragon just shook her head when she walked by his chair. The bell finally rang.

Freedom! Derrick thought.

After school, practice ended almost before he knew it. Derrick worked hard, running and dodging the offensive linemen. He tried to keep his mouth shut too.

On his way out of the locker room, Coach Harris stopped him.

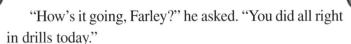

"How's it going, Farley?" he asked. "You did all right in drills today."

Derrick looked Coach in the eyes. "Fine," he fibbed.

"I talked with Mrs. Dowling at lunch today," Coach said. "It's not looking too good, is it?"

Derrick's heart sank.

"She says you're not stepping up to the plate," Coach went on. "She mentioned you have a big paper coming up. Are you working on it?"

"Uh, yes. Well, sort of. I mean, I've started," Derrick stammered.

"I thought you cared about the team, Derrick." Coach shook his head in disappointment.

"Uh, yes, Coach," Derrick mumbled. "I do."

"Then you'd better show it," Coach said. "Get home and do your essay."

"Okay," Derrick agreed. "But I have to go to work first."

Coach looked at Derrick. "The team is depending on you, you know. Shape up!"

Derrick stood rooted to the spot. Here we go again! he thought. He needed to get out of here—and fast.

"Sure, Coach," he said. "I have to go."

"I hope you're watching that mouth of yours at work too," Coach added.

"Yes, Coach," Derrick managed to choke out. "See ya," he tossed back over his shoulder as he hustled out the doors.

Blah, blah, blah, Derrick said to himself as he tied his red apron on at Taste of Italy. Everyone was after him. Why didn't anyone understand? What was life without a couple of jokes?

He wiped down tables. Then he walked back into the kitchen to get silverware.

"I have to meet with a pasta salesman in the dining room," Joe told him. "Will you watch the lasagna noodles for me?"

"Uh-huh," Derrick agreed. He took the spoon from Joe.

"Take them out when they're done. Then drain them," Joe instructed. "Make sure you don't tear them."

"Uh-huh," Derrick answered. Geez, this wasn't rocket science, was it? he joked to himself.

Joe walked back through the double doors into the dining room.

"Pay attention," Craig warned. He stood at the chopping block. Thwack! Thwack! His knife sliced onions.

Derrick made an ugly face at Craig when he turned his back.

He fished out a lasagna noodle with the tongs. First it had to cool off before he could test it. He didn't want to be breathing flames like Dowling the Dragon.

"Just right!" he said after swallowing a bite.

He scooped out the noodles and dumped them in the strainer. The noodles looked like huge bandages.

Hah! A thought burst into his brain. Picking up three noodles, he ran them under cool water. Then he plastered them across his face like huge bandages. He draped them over his ears.

"A mummy!" Derrick croaked. He began stalking toward Craig, his arms stretched out in front of him. "Direct from the grave! Fear for your life!" he howled.

Craig wheeled around. Just then, the double doors swished open.

*"Che cosa fái?"* Joe thundered out. "What do you think you're doing?"

Derrick gulped. Blood rushed to his forehead. He pulled the lasagna noodles off his face.

"N—n—nothing!" he exclaimed, rubbing his face hard. The noodles were sticky.

"I'm trying to run a business here," Joe fumed. He shook a fist at Derrick. "How am I going to get new customers when my busboy is wearing my noodles?"

"Uh, sorry! It won't happen again! I—I just couldn't help it!" Derrick stammered. From the corner of his eye, he saw Craig's furious face.

"One more chance," Joe threatened. "You get one more

chance. That's it. And that's only because you've worked well so far. And because of your brother." He stared at Derrick. "If I lose any customers because of you, you're gone."

Derrick's forehead broke out in a sweat. That would be all he'd need. Mom and Dad would be all over him.

"Okay, okay," Derrick said quickly. He lunged for the silverware and napkins. "I'm on my way."

"Don't kill yourself rushing to the dining room," Joe grunted. "Hardly anyone is here."

Derrick trudged out to the dining room. Only one couple sat at a table. The restaurant looked big—and empty.

Craig followed him, right on his heels.

"Listen!" he snarled.

Derrick backed up against a table.

Craig went on. "Stop goofing around." Craig thrust his face right into Derrick's. "Joe's a good guy. He'll starve if we don't get any new business. And I'll lose my job. I need money for college. And here you are acting like it's *Comedy Corner.*"

"Okay, okay," Derrick agreed. "I'll do better."

"Do *better*!" Craig scoffed. "You'd better do something *right* for a change!" He stomped back into the kitchen.

Derrick glared at the doors closing behind Craig. What a meathead! Then he frowned. But you'd better shape up, he told himself. Unless he wanted everything to come crashing down on him, he'd better try to do something right.

He'd *try* anyway.

# cHapter Five

# YOU TaLKiN' to Me?

Derrick walked home from Taste of Italy after his shift. He sniffed his shirt. It smelled like garlic. At least it didn't smell as bad as Dowling the Dragon's breath. He snorted to himself.

Craig would be home later. Derrick groaned. What would Craig tell Mom and Dad about the lasagna mummy?

Derrick mumbled hello to his parents as he walked through the living room.

"Everything okay, Derrick?" Mom asked, looking up from the TV.

Dad looked at Derrick. Derrick couldn't meet his eyes.

"Uh-huh," Derrick answered. "I'm just tired. I have homework to do."

Derrick walked into the room he shared with Craig. He pulled out the English assignment and lay down on his bed. Maybe if he closed his eyes, everything would go away.

Why did Mom and Dad have to be home? He'd sure like to pop a copy of *The Brothers* or *Wayne's World* in the VCR and watch it. It would help him relax.

Nah, he'd never be able to relax. Everyone was on his case. He'd better get to work.

He began reading the article on doctors. Then he read one on health insurance. Geez! he thought. The health-care system was really messed up. And the patients were getting the shaft. Derrick shook his head.

Craig's voice sounded from the living room. He must have just gotten home from Taste of Italy. A worried frown creased Derrick's forehead. Now what?

Suddenly, the door to his room flung open. Dad stood in the doorway. Next to him, Mom folded her arms. He could see Craig's smug face behind them. *Gee thanks, snitch,* Derrick wanted to spit out.

"You have some explaining to do," Dad demanded.

"It's bad enough that you risked your own job—a job you need. How could you risk Craig's job too?" Mom asked. "Or hurt business for Joe? That's not very thoughtful or mature."

Against his will, Derrick felt his face turn red. Craig's face looked triumphant.

"The mummy!" Dad exclaimed in disgust. "How could you do that?"

"You're too intelligent to act that way," Mom added.

Derrick hung his head. *But it's fun*, he wanted to protest. He had to have fun, right?

"Think about it," Mom said. "Times are tough. It's time to grow up, Derrick."

With a look of disappointment, his parents turned and left him alone.

*Times are tough. Grow up.* His parents' words echoed in his brain all night. He tossed and turned. Thumping his pillow, he rolled over again to try to sleep.

But he still couldn't help making a few silent jokes. Grow up, he repeated. He imagined himself growing seven feet tall. "Have I grown up enough?" he'd ask. Derrick muffled his laughter in his pillow.

English class came too soon Friday. The class straggled into the computer lab. Rod picked a chair next to Derrick's.

"Let's get started on rough drafts today," Dowling the Dragon instructed them. "This paper is due next Thursday."

Derrick sighed. He turned on the computer. Sure, he'd finished the articles last night. He'd even scribbled some notes on his outline. But what could he really write about?

He stared in despair at the computer screen. The cursor blinked.

Suddenly, Derrick snapped to attention. The cursor was moving across the screen. It was typing! He rubbed his eyes. What?

**What's up? A funny guy, eh?** the computer typed across the screen. **Yeah, sure. Smart off to your parents. Smart off to your teacher, your boss, and your coach. But you're really a loser. That's right, L-O-S-E-R!**

Derrick felt the blood drain from his face. Someone was messing with him! Fury bubbled up inside. He peered behind the computer. He didn't see anything unusual.

He stood up and began stalking through the aisles. Was someone else networked with him? Was one of his buddies doing this? Were they sending messages to his computer? He studied everyone's screens. They were all typing their own sentences about health care.

"Derrick? Need a little break from all your hard work?" Dowling the Dragon's voice sliced through the air.

"Uh, yeah," Derrick said. He slunk back to his chair. What was going on?

Rod glanced over. Derrick shook his head and made a face. Rod grinned and went on typing.

L-O-S-E-R! The word still glowed on the screen. It taunted him. He'd like to punch a hole right through the screen. Derrick rubbed his fist. No, that would hurt.

Maybe he could just pull the plug. He began to reach for the power cord.

Ah-ah-ah! the computer typed. Step away from the computer! Repeat! Step away from the computer! This is a warning.

Derrick stiffened. The stupid thing knew what he was doing! He whipped his head around. Could anyone else see what was going on?

What should he do? What if Dowling the Dragon stomped down the aisle? She'd think he'd written some trash. He'd have detention for sure.

He had to get rid of this. Somehow, he had to make the computer stop.

**Who's in there?** he typed quickly.

**You have a smart mouth, don't you? Why don't you write like that?** the cursor tapped out.

"Huh?" Derrick said aloud. "What?"

Next to him, Rod looked over. His eyebrows were raised in a question. Derrick tried to look casual. He shrugged his shoulders.

"Must be good," Rod joked.

"Yeah," Derrick said.

Rod grinned and went back to typing.

On the screen, the cursor blinked at Derrick.

"What are you doing to me?" Derrick hissed at it.

Blink! Blink! Blink!

"Okay," Derrick muttered through clenched teeth. So the computer couldn't hear him. He'd better type it in.

**What are you doing to me? Who are you?** His fingers raced over the keyboard.

**Your sick brain! Ha! Ha!** the computer sneered.

Blood pounded in Derrick's forehead. He cracked his knuckles.

He swiveled his head around to look at his classmates. No one was paying attention. Dowling the Dragon was across the room. No doubt she was flaming the back of some poor kid's neck with her evil breath.

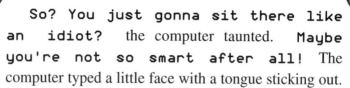

**So? You just gonna sit there like an idiot?** the computer taunted. **Maybe you're not so smart after all!** The computer typed a little face with a tongue sticking out.

**Stop it!** Derrick typed in quickly. He hoped that no one was looking over his shoulder.

**So write something. Bet you can't!** the cursor jeered. **You have nothing to say. You can't even use your smarts to write something smart. Sure, you have a quick mouth. But are you quick on paper?**

**Watch me!** Derrick typed furiously. He *did* have some ideas. He *was* smart.

Derrick slid the mouse across the mouse pad. He clicked at the top of the screen. The cursor began blinking. The screen went blank. Whew!

He took a deep breath and glanced at his scribbled outline. Here goes nothing, he told himself.

**Health insurance companies have pushed people around for a long time,** he typed. He sat back from the computer. Hmm—not too bad, he thought.

Derrick flexed his fingers over the keyboard. **The companies think people zoom off to the hospital for any nick or scratch.**

Yes! Derrick told himself. **Take that!** he typed in at the bottom of the screen.

He looked around quickly. No one better be watching him "talk" to his computer. Derrick shook his head to clear it.

Talking to the computer—was he crazy?

## CHAPTER SIX

# Hanging by a Threat

The bell rang, signaling the end of English class. Derrick jerked in surprise. Class was over already? he asked himself. He leaned back in his chair.

He groaned as he stretched out his arms. He'd been hunched forward concentrating on his typing. His fingers almost had cramps in them. He flexed them. Pulling the sheets of paper from the printer, he tucked them into his backpack.

Derrick reached to shut off the computer. As he leaned toward it, the cursor blinked.

`That's a start, Mr. Funny Man. Let's see if you can keep it up.`

"Aaaaaargh!" Derrick moaned and flipped the switch. Twink! The light vanished from the screen.

Whew, he thought. He turned to Rod.

"Let's get to football," Derrick said. "We have to win today." He scooped up his backpack.

The two boys threaded their way through the aisles. Shaun joined them.

"I hope you got something worthwhile done today, Derrick," Mrs. Dowling called out.

"Uh-huh," Derrick said. He hurried out the door.

"Let's move," he urged Rod and Shaun. "I don't want to breathe dragon fumes just before the game." He grinned wickedly. "It would make my legs like jelly."

Rod and Shaun hooted and howled. They clapped Derrick on the back.

"You're bad," Shaun said. His grin spread across his face.

"Yeah, hope I'm bad on the football field too," Derrick said. "Coach better not bench me. My dad is getting off work today for the game."

"You'll play," Rod encouraged. "You're the man."

The first half of the game passed in a blur. Derrick sat on the bench. Upset, he rested his chin in his hands. He felt as if steam were curling up from his ears. Every now and then, he'd pound his fist into his open palm. Staring at Coach Harris didn't get him on the field either.

On the field, Ricardo went out for a pass. The ball almost glided into his arms. Everyone jumped up and yelled when he blasted across the goal line. Derrick clenched his fists tighter.

He didn't dare look up in the bleachers. Dad would give him that look. Of course, he could guess what Dad would be thinking. *Did you open your mouth again, Derrick?* Derrick shrank down inside his football pads.

Finally, after halftime, Coach called, "Farley! You're in!"

Derrick raced onto the field and joined the huddle. Serious business now, he told himself. He had to score, or he wouldn't be playing much again.

In a low voice, Shaun called out the play. They broke the huddle and hustled to their positions on the field.

TWEEEEET! The referee's whistle blew.

Snap! Thud! Shaun caught the ball. He fell back. The linemen blocked for him.

Derrick went out for the pass, zigzagging toward

the sideline. He kept his eye on Shaun. A defensive back tried to cover him. He shadowed Derrick's moves.

Derrick grunted, shoving into the player. Derrick kept his balance and continued running.

Now! Derrick gave a final burst of speed, outrunning another player trying to cover him. The ball spiraled toward him. With open arms, Derrick leaped up and snagged the ball out of the air.

Cradling the ball in his arm, he raced down the sideline. He dodged a couple of tackles. Finally, the end zone was in sight. His breath came in ragged bursts. He had to do this.

Sprinting as if his life depended on it, Derrick dove across the goal line. A huge defensive player just missed mowing him down. The player thudded onto the grass just behind Derrick.

TWEEEEET! The referee's whistle shrilled. He flung his arms up in the touchdown sign.

Fans in the bleachers cheered and howled. Derrick's teammates jumped on him gleefully.

"Way to go, man!"

"You did it again!"

"You're the man!"

Derrick grinned. Yes! He'd proven himself—to his coach, to his parents, to his teammates, to himself.

After the game, the team showered and dressed. Coach Harris grabbed Derrick just inside the locker room doors.

"Know why you played only half the game again today?" he quizzed Derrick.

Water from his wet hair dripped down Derrick's face. He tightened his grip on his old football shoes and blinked at Coach.

Derrick sighed. "Uh, I guess so," he admitted.

"And why would that be? Why would I be benching the most talented wide receiver in the league two games in a row?" Coach Harris asked. He thumped his clipboard against his side.

"Uh, because of my smart mouth in practice," Derrick mumbled. He stared down at the floor.

"I'll tell you what," Coach said. "You find a way to use that smart mouth productively—*and* work hard to stay eligible." He clapped Derrick on the back. "Then I'll play you every chance I get. The high school coach will be watching for upcoming talent." He looked long and hard at Derrick. "That could be you if you shape up."

"Uh-huh, Coach," Derrick agreed. "Thanks." He hurried out the doors to meet his dad.

*Yeah, thanks a lot,* Derrick repeated to himself. *Thanks for being on my case. Thanks for benching me for half the game. Thanks for nothing.*

Derrick lifted his chin. At least Coach said he'd play him. And the high school coach would be watching.

"Good game, son," Dad said. "Great run."

"Thanks, Dad," Derrick said. A little burst of hope filled him. Maybe Dad hadn't noticed he hadn't played the first half. Then maybe he wouldn't get the millionth lecture on his smart mouth. Forget it, Derrick admitted to himself. Dad would nail him.

"Do you want to tell me why you were on the bench for the first half?" Dad asked.

They got to the car in the parking lot. Holding back a sigh, Derrick opened his door. He tossed his backpack into the backseat and slid into the front seat.

"Ah, well, you know," Derrick stammered.

"No," Dad retorted. "You tell me."

Derrick clicked the seat belt together. He swallowed hard. "Coach thinks I need to be benched. He thinks it might help me to remember to keep my mouth shut," Derrick admitted.

Dad wheeled the car out of the lot. He glanced over at Derrick. His eyebrows raised.

Derrick just stared out the window at the passing cars.

"If you're doing your so-called comedy act at practice, it's no wonder you're in trouble," Dad said. He braked at a red light.

"But . . . but that's who I am!" Derrick protested.

"And look where it's gotten you," Dad responded. "On the bench."

Derrick tightened his mouth.

"Your mother and I have warned you," Dad said. "You're hanging by a thread here."

"You mean hanging by a *threat*, right?" Derrick couldn't help blurting out. Then he winced at Dad's expression.

Dad shook his head. "I don't know, Derrick," he said. "Someday you'll figure it out. And you'd better do it sooner than later."

The next day, Derrick washed his hands in the kitchen at Taste of Italy. He'd finally gotten into the routine. It wasn't that tough of a job. Wipe the tables. Set them. Clear the tables when customers were done. Help Craig with the dishes. Help out with the simple cooking. It was pretty easy.

Joe treated him okay too. Now if only Craig would lay off.

"At least you're on time," Craig grudgingly admitted today. He swirled a huge spoon in some red sauce bubbling on the stove.

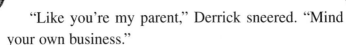 

"Like you're my parent," Derrick sneered. "Mind your own business."

"*You* mind your mouth," Craig snapped back. He slapped the spoon down in the pot. The sauce spattered his glasses.

"Hah!" Derrick hooted. "Serves you right."

"Try growing up sometime," Craig retorted. He wiped his glasses off with a clean rag.

"You first," Derrick taunted. He grinned. Craig rolled his eyes and turned his back on Derrick.

Derrick glanced into the dining room. Hardly anyone was here again, he realized. Frowning, he rubbed his hands dry. Picking up the spray cleaner and a rag, he pushed through the doors. He stopped suddenly.

Joe sat at a table in the corner. A stack of bills lay in front of him. His head was bent over a list of figures. A worried frown creased his forehead.

"What's up, Joe?" Derrick asked.

Joe's head snapped up. He blinked at Derrick. "Oh, just more bills than I want," he complained. He gestured at the empty restaurant. "We have our loyal customers from our old location coming back. But we need new ones to fill up this place. We have to get the word out. But I can't afford advertising."

"That's too bad," Derrick said. "I keep telling all my friends. Maybe they'll come with their families," he added hopefully.

"Good job," Joe said. "We sure could use the business." He sank his chin on his hands. "We were busting out of my old place. I thought for sure more people would come once I moved in here."

"Oh, yeah," Derrick said. "Like *Field of Dreams*, that old movie? Remember? There it was 'Build it and they will come.' Here it's 'Rent it and they will come.' "

A weak smile crept across Joe's face. "Something like that, yes," he agreed. Then he shook his head. "What worries me is having to let you go—and maybe even Craig," he added.

Derrick frowned a little. "You mean, you think you'll have to fire us?" he asked.

Joe leaned back in the chair. He rubbed the back of his neck.

"I don't want to," he said. "But if business doesn't pick up in the next month, I may have to. I signed a year's lease on this place. I have to hang on until then. And I can't afford to pay both of you *and* the rent."

Derrick stared at Joe. "But what can we do? I need this job."

"And I need the business," Joe said. "We just have to figure out how to get it."

The chimes over the restaurant door rang out. A family with three kids walked in. The first early birds! Derrick thought. Maybe this will be the day the place got busy.

Joe sprang up from his table. Smiling, he grabbed some menus.

Derrick quickly began cleaning tables. As he wiped, questions ran through his head. How could he help Joe get more customers? He shrugged helplessly. What could he do? After all, he was just a guy with a smart mouth.

Later that night, Derrick stared at his backpack lying on his bed. Had he been imagining all that stuff with the computer? he wondered. No way could a computer talk to somebody, he taunted himself.

More important, had he really written okay stuff for the essay? Quickly, he searched through the papers in his binder. He yanked out his English assignment.

He read the first paragraph. Not bad, he congratulated himself. It sounded like the way he talked to his buddies. Somehow the computer had made him write like that.

Then Derrick stared at the last page he'd worked on. A feeling of dread ran through him. How would he finish it? He'd been on a roll today. But now, his mind was blank again.

He decided he'd wait until Monday. Then he'd head to the computer lab, turn on the computer, and . . .

And what? he asked himself. What if the computer was silent?

## CHapter Seven

# Keyboard Crazy

Sunday afternoon, Derrick walked out of the dark movie theater. He blinked in the sunlight. Shaun and Rod were shoving each other and laughing.

"*You* did!" Rod howled.

"Nah—*you* did!" Shaun disagreed. He gave Rod a fake punch.

"Uh-uh," Derrick countered. He stopped walking and looked at his friends. He folded his arms. "You *both* acted like morons with those girls," he teased. "What was up with the popcorn stuff? You're lucky the usher didn't throw you out!" Derrick pretended to frown and sighed dramatically. "You young men need to grow up!"

"Yeah? Who's talking about growing up?" Shaun challenged. "The funny man of Walker Middle School? Mr. Mess Around?"

"Yeah," Rod agreed. "We're just following your example!" He and Shaun elbowed each other and bumped fists. "Mr. Adult!" Rod teased.

"Hey," Derrick said. They headed to the bus stop. "I'm not that bad," he protested. "I just like to joke around a little."

"Yeah," Shaun said. "Right. Dowling the Dragon sure likes your jokes too. Maybe she'll give you a good grade for jokes on your essay." He grinned. "That's okay though," he joked. "We don't really need you on the football team. We can win the league without you," he said. "Ricardo wants your position anyway."

Derrick flinched. "I'm working on it, okay?" he said. "I'm writing the paper."

The bus pulled up to the curb. Derrick bounded up the steps. He knew Shaun was kidding, but his words still stung. What if he really did get kicked out of football?

He frowned. Then there was the Taste of Italy problem. He couldn't lose his job. He needed new football shoes. Even worse, Mom and Dad were counting on him to work.

Derrick plopped down on the bus seat. He leaned his head back. There was too much going on in his life. Why couldn't he just crack jokes and hang with his buddies?

Monday afternoon, Derrick walked into the computer lab. He dropped down in the chair in front of his computer. The blank screen made him swallow hard. What would it do today?

"Good afternoon, class," Mrs. Dowling said. "You have a lot of work to do today. Your essays are due this Thursday. Then we'll get started on your next paper. It will be a creative short story."

A creative short story? Derrick almost groaned aloud. He'd thought he'd be off the hook when this health-care essay was done.

Dowling the Dragon paused. Was she looking at him? Derrick wondered. He scrunched down in his chair.

"Get going," she warned.

Derrick turned on the computer. The screen lit up. His hand slid the mouse to click on the word processing program. His heart beat a little faster.

The cursor blinked on the screen. Derrick tensed. It wasn't saying anything.

Reaching into his backpack, he grabbed the disk. He slid it into the disk drive and clicked on the file.

He scanned his essay—what there was of it. Now what?

**What's up?** The cursor suddenly flickered across the screen.

Derrick jumped in surprise. He swiveled his head around. Was anyone watching? No one seemed to be looking his way. All he heard was the clack-clack of keyboards.

Next to him, Shaun was busy typing. He looked over at Derrick.

"*I'm* not going to flunk English," Shaun bragged. He flexed his biceps. "I'll be out on the field." He grinned at Derrick.

"Yeah?" Derrick said. "I will too. Just wait till you read this."

Then he wanted to kick himself. What was he saying? In horror, he watched Shaun lean toward his screen.

Quickly, Derrick held up his rough draft, covering the screen.

"Not yet," he said. "Not until it's finished."

"Afraid I'll copy your golden words?" Shaun taunted.

"Yeah," Derrick sneered. "You wish."

Shaun turned back to his computer. From the corner of his eye, Derrick watched Shaun until he started working again. Whew, he thought. That was close.

He pulled the paper away from the screen. The computer had typed something else.

**Hey! I can't see anything! What do you think you're doing?**

Derrick just stared at the screen.

**You look down today,** the cursor tapped out.

Derrick glanced around the class again. Dowling the Dragon was reading something on someone's screen. The poor kid was probably choking on dragon-breath fumes. He snorted silently.

**I have too much junk on my mind.** Derrick typed quickly. **Everybody's hassling me.**

**It wouldn't be because of that attitude, would it?** the computer asked.

Derrick frowned. **Get over it,** he typed. **I have other problems too. I might lose my job.**

**Your smart mouth keeping the customers away?** the cursor typed.

Derrick wanted to punch his fist through the screen. What was the computer's problem?

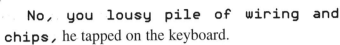

**No, you lousy pile of wiring and chips,** he tapped on the keyboard.

**&#@%!** the cursor blinked.

Derrick grinned.

**Taste of Italy is losing business. It's not my fault,** Derrick typed.

**Why don't you use your smart mouth to get customers in the door?** the computer asked.

"Huh?" Derrick said aloud. Shaun glanced over and shrugged. Derrick flushed. He moved the monitor a little to block Shaun's view of the screen.

**What do you mean?** Derrick typed in. **Tell them jokes or something? That's lame.**

**If no one knows about the restaurant, they won't come,** the cursor blinked. **Make up a flyer. Make it funny. Hand it out on the streets.**

**Me?** Derrick typed in. He almost squawked it aloud.

**Yeah, you! If you want to be a stand-up comedian, you need to have confidence. Here's your chance. Use your comedy to lure customers to the restaurant. Try it and see what happens.**

Make a funny flyer? Derrick repeated silently. It wasn't a *bad* idea. Maybe he could make up a rap or something.

It wouldn't be that hard handing them out either. He could do it some day after practice when he didn't have to work.

**Well? Are you stepping up to the plate or not?** the computer taunted.

**Yeah, yeah, yeah. Okay,** Derrick typed.

**So get started!** the computer ordered.

Derrick checked out the room. Dowling the Dragon was four aisles away. He was still safe.

He leaned back in his chair and closed his eyes. Hah! An idea burst into his brain.

He clicked to a new screen. Flexing his fingers over the keyboard, he began to type. He could get this flyer done quickly and then work on his essay.

**Just follow your nose. Come to Joe's.** His fingers flew over the keys.

**That rhymes. Not bad,** the computer replied. **You need more though.**

"Yeah, yeah," Derrick muttered. He kept typing. **Don't be chicken. Your fingers you'll be lickin'.**

**That's weak,** the cursor typed out.

Derrick made a face at the screen. **What do *you* know?** he typed in.

`More than you,` the computer sneered back.

Hitting the delete key, Derrick took a breath. The sentence vanished.

Okay, he told himself. He rubbed his hands together.

`Walk in our door. You'll be asking for more,` he typed. He made the type larger. **`JOE'S TASTE OF ITALY—THE BEST GARLIC` ~~`BREATH`~~`-OOPS-BREAD IN TOWN`**`.` He finished and grinned.

`That should get people's attention anyway,` the cursor commented.

A hand suddenly gripped Derrick's shoulder. He froze.

"And what have we here?" Mrs. Dowling's tone sent a chill down his spine. Busted! he moaned to himself.

"The best garlic breath—oops—bread in town?" Icicles dripped from her words. "What does this have to do with health care?" she asked.

"Ah . . . ah . . ." Derrick fumbled for words. "I just had this idea," he fibbed, "for the creative short story that's next." He was on a roll now, he congratulated himself. "I had to get it down before I forgot it—just like you always say to do. It's about a . . . a comedian who owns a pizza joint."

Mrs. Dowling sighed. She took her hand off his shoulder. Her nasty dragon claws had almost ripped his shirt, he joked silently.

"Hmm," she said sarcastically. "Right. You'd better get to work on the health-care essay," she warned.

"Yes, ma'am," Derrick said.

"And, Derrick," the Dragon continued.

"Yes, ma'am," he answered.

"Cut the 'ma'am' baloney," she snapped. "It doesn't fool anyone, least of all me." She stalked away.

Shaun looked over and grinned. Derrick grinned back. Whew!

The flyer actually looked pretty good. He enlarged the type again. Then he turned the printer on. Mrs. Dowling was terrorizing some other poor kid across the room now.

He pushed **print** and **50** for copies. The printer began clacking out the flyers. He kept glancing around nervously. He'd be in huge trouble if he got caught.

Yes! he told himself when the last flyer was printed. No one seemed to be paying any attention to him. That was good, he told himself. No one would believe his health-care essay was 50 pages long!

He planned to hand the flyers out on his way home after practice today. He'd hit the dry cleaners, the little market, the shoe-repair shop, the gift shop, and the newsstand. He'd try out some comedy routines on people too. Maybe he could even come up with some good jokes about Italian food.

**Come on, you slacker!** the computer blinked. **Write the essay. Or you may be working full-time at Taste of Italy when you flunk out of school.**

**VERY FUNNY! HAH, HAH!** Derrick typed in.

**Don't shout at me,** the computer retorted.

Derrick shook his head. He clicked back to his essay screen. The ideas began to flow again.

Before he knew it, the bell rang. "That's it for today," Mrs. Dowling announced.

Derrick saved his work on his disk. Then he printed out a copy. He slipped it into his backpack.

**Shape up in football practice too,** the computer flashed at him.

**You're worse than my parents,** Derrick complained.

**You're in deep trouble already,** the cursor typed out. **You should be thanking me—and kissing my screen.**

**Yeah, right. Sick,** Derrick typed in. **Gotta go.**

**Then go,** the computer blinked.

Was he nuts? Derrick asked himself. Now he had a computer telling him what to do. He clicked off the computer.

Twink! The screen went dark.

After football practice, Rod, Shaun, and Derrick packed their gear into their gym bags.

"You feeling all right?" Rod asked Derrick.

Derrick shrugged. "Yeah? Why?" he asked.

Together, they walked out of the locker room. A breeze was blowing some fall leaves around.

"You were kind of quiet today in practice," Shaun said. He reached out his hand to feel Derrick's forehead. "Do you have a fever?" he asked with a grin.

Derrick batted Shaun's hand away. "Get away from me!" he joked.

Shaun just laughed.

"I'm fine," Derrick continued. "I just want to be sure I play. Coach Harris gave me the word. The high school coach will be watching some of the games. So I *have* to be playing."

"Makes sense," Shaun said. "Now all you need to do is stay eligible."

Derrick's heart sank. "Yeah, I know."

In his backpack, he could feel the weight of the flyers. He had to give those out on his way home.

"And I have to keep my job too," Derrick went on. "My parents won't let me play if I'm not working."

He kicked an empty pop can. It rolled along the sidewalk.

"Why?" Rod asked.

"Something about growing up. If I'm not mature enough for a job, I'm not mature enough to play football," Derrick grumbled. "Plus they want me to start paying for extra things, like my football shoes."

"Wow!" Shaun hooted. "They really are on your case."

"Uh-huh," Derrick agreed. The bus rolled up. "I'm going to walk home," he said. "I have stuff to do."

"You're not meeting those girls from the movie, are you?" Shaun teased.

Derrick laughed. "Not today," he said. "Besides, I wouldn't want any girls that would look at you two clowns."

"Hey," Shaun protested.

"Maybe we'll come by work tomorrow," Rod said. "Get you some points with your boss. You know, more customers."

"Yeah," Shaun agreed.

Derrick flinched. "Uh, that might not be a good idea," he said quickly.

"Why? We wouldn't get you in trouble again," Shaun said, elbowing Rod.

"Still, you'd better not," Derrick said.

"Okay," Shaun said. "Whatever you say." Derrick saw him look at Rod, raising his eyebrows.

They said their good-byes. Derrick began walking down the street. He headed into the dry cleaners first.

"Sure," the woman behind the counter said. She read the flyer aloud and laughed. " 'Best garlic breath—oops—bread in town!' " she said, smiling. "That's good. I'll have to go eat there myself. How about a dozen flyers? I'll be sure to hand them out."

"Thanks," Derrick said. He smiled. Maybe this would work. Maybe more people *would* go to Joe's.

Derrick winced. As long as it wasn't Shaun and Rod who walked in. That was all he needed.

But if the flyers made business get better, maybe he could keep his job. Then his parents would let him keep playing football.

Of course, he still had to get a good grade on his essay.

## CHapter Eight

# RUN to DayLight

Wednesday, Derrick hunched over the computer in English. In a frenzy, his fingers raced over the keys. He'd already written his rough draft. Over the last two days, he'd scribbled more changes.

This was his final copy. The paper was due tomorrow. He had to finish. And if he didn't get at least a B, he was doomed.

**Ouch!** the cursor blinked at him. **Quit typing so fast!**

Derrick grinned. **That's what you wanted, wasn't it?** he typed in. **Gotcha!**

**#$%&*!** the computer replied.

Derrick chuckled.

Next to him, Shaun leaned over.

"What's up?" he asked. "Are you talking to that computer?"

"Nah," Derrick fibbed quickly. "I was just talking to myself. It helps me think better."

"Weird, man," Shaun said, shaking his head. He returned to his own typing.

Derrick finished up his last sentence. Yes! he thought. He pressed **print.** The printer began spitting out the sheets of paper.

"Not too bad," Derrick bragged.

"Yeah?" Shaun asked. "It better be like that Shakespeare guy, or you'll be off the football team."

Derrick winced. Holding his paper out to Shaun, he said, "Read this."

All around him, he could hear printers clack-clacking out students' papers. Everyone was in a rush. Dowling the Dragon had no mercy. She lowered grades for late papers.

Shaun read slowly, his forehead crinkling. He looked up at Derrick.

"You really wrote this, didn't you? It even sounds like the way you talk. I didn't know you could write like this," he admitted. "It's funny—but it kind of says something too." Shaun shook his head. "I just hope Mrs. Dowling likes it."

Derrick's smile faded. "Yeah," he said. "Me too."

Across the room, Mrs. Dowling was leaning over a computer, scolding a student. Maybe she wouldn't like it, Derrick groaned silently. Maybe the computer had tricked him into making a fool of himself. He'd have a tough time explaining *that* to everyone.

The bell rang. At least he'd finished. He could turn in his paper on time tomorrow. He stapled his two pages together. Slipping them into his backpack, he stood up.

"Let's go, Mr. Funny Man," Shaun teased. Derrick punched him lightly on the arm.

The next day in English, Mrs. Dowling looked at the class over the top of her glasses.

"Take out your essays, ladies and gentlemen," she said.

She stared right at Derrick. Derrick tried to stare right back at her. Don't blink, he commanded himself. Wasn't this how dragons killed all those knights? Staring them down with their evil eyes? Well, she wouldn't get *him*! At least not that way.

"This is an important assignment. Your grade will matter a great deal," the Dragon was saying. "For some of you even more than others," she added meaningfully.

Derrick shifted uneasily in his desk. He pulled out his essay and passed it forward. From the next desk, Shaun leaned over.

"Good luck, bro," he whispered.

"Thanks," Derrick answered. He watched his paper make its way up the row. Go, little buddy, he encouraged it silently. Maybe it could charm Dowling the Dragon into giving him a C-. He couldn't do anything now. It was all up to the Dragon.

After football practice, Coach walked into the locker room.

"Farley?" he called out.

Derrick looked up from zipping his bag. Did Coach look angry?

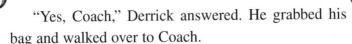

"Yes, Coach," Derrick answered. He grabbed his bag and walked over to Coach.

Coach Harris reached around behind Derrick. He yanked down the bill of Derrick's cap and grinned.

"I just wanted you to know that I've been impressed with you all week," he said.

Derrick's mouth dropped open.

"You've been cooperative. You've worked hard. You've been a good team player. And you've kept that mouth shut." Coach paused. "So . . ." he stretched out, ". . . you'll be starting tomorrow."

Derrick's heart lifted. "Thanks, Coach," he said.

"And the high school coach tells me he'll be watching the game," Coach added.

"All right!" Derrick exclaimed.

"So score tomorrow," Coach threatened. "Or you'll look bad in front of a lot of people."

"No problem," Derrick said. "I'll work on it."

All the way to Taste of Italy, Derrick couldn't stop grinning. People stared at him. They must think he was an idiot, he told himself, as he walked up Watt Avenue. But he didn't care. He was starting tomorrow—and the high school coach would be there.

Derrick stopped in front of the dry cleaners. Wait. What if he blew his chance? He stared at the ground. Coach would have to put in Ricardo at least for a while. What if Ricardo looked better at his position than he did?

Derrick straightened his shoulders and kept walking. No way. He'd play his best. He'd run and dodge and blast his way across the goal line no matter what.

Derrick reached for the door at Taste of Italy. Then he stopped. Would there be more customers today? When he opened the door, would a ton of people be waiting in line? His flyer must have helped, right?

Hoping against hope, Derrick opened the door. His spirits sank. Only two tables were full. The restaurant was almost empty. His great flyer hadn't done anything.

Had it made people angry? Derrick wondered. Nah, that couldn't be. They probably just thought it was dumb—like his jokes.

Derrick put away his school stuff and washed up. He was ready for another night of work.

"Hello, Derrick," Joe called from the back of the kitchen. "Did you bring some customers with you?" he joked.

"I wish," Derrick replied, trying to sound cheerful. He couldn't help noticing that Joe's face looked tired. The bills must be getting to him.

For the first time, Derrick worried about Joe as well as himself. What would happen to Joe if the restaurant didn't make it? Derrick wouldn't be the only one out of a job.

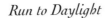

Friday's English class came too soon. Derrick sat down in his desk. He looked uneasily at Dowling the Dragon. Had she read his paper yet?

"I haven't been able to read all your papers yet," Mrs. Dowling said. "But I *can* say that some of them are quite good."

She smiled at Neena, who always got an A. Derrick held back a sigh. Why couldn't she look at *him* when she said that?

Mrs. Dowling's mouth stretched into a dragon smile, showing her pointy teeth. "And some of them are . . . quite different," she said.

Derrick shrank down in his desk. What did that mean? Was 'different' dragon language for F?

Derrick barely paid attention through the rest of class. Thoughts of the upcoming football game filled his head. He could just see himself racing for the goal line. He imagined the high school coach taking notes in the stands. *Farley—good potential*, the coach would write. That was how coaches talked, wasn't it? Derrick clenched his hands into fists. He had to score.

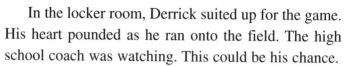 

In the locker room, Derrick suited up for the game. His heart pounded as he ran onto the field. The high school coach was watching. This could be his chance.

The minutes passed quickly. Toward the end of the game, the score was tied.

A few seconds before the final whistle, Shaun lofted a pass high in the air. Watching it spiral, Derrick sprinted down the field. He grunted, dodging a defender. Losing his balance, the defensive player tumbled onto the field.

Arms outstretched, Derrick leaped into the air. Got it! The ball fell safely into his hands. He tucked it under his arm. He twisted away from one tackler and then another. He blew across the last remaining yards before the goal line.

"Yeah!" Shaun hollered. Derrick's teammates ran down the field. They jumped on him, wrestling him to the ground. The stands cheered.

Derrick congratulated himself as he picked himself up off the field. His buddies clapped him on the back. He'd done it. He'd proven himself. And Coach Harris would play him—as long as he kept his mouth shut.

Would he make the high school team next year? Derrick asked himself Saturday afternoon as he walked to Taste of Italy. That would be great. But what about the rest of this year? Would he get to keep playing?

Derrick shuffled his feet as he walked. Fallen leaves crunched under his feet.

Derrick turned the corner and stopped. His mouth dropped open. A small cluster of people stood outside Taste of Italy. What was wrong? Was there a problem inside?

"Excuse me," Derrick said, threading his way through the people. He pushed open the door.

A wave of noise greeted him. At least a dozen people packed the waiting area. The tables were filling up. Craig was almost running from table to table, menus in hand.

Joe stood at the entrance to the dining room. He looked worried. He was explaining something to some waiting customers. He gestured with his hands.

Joe looked up and saw Derrick. He frowned and began squeezing through the crowd toward Derrick.

Derrick saw Joe was holding something in his hand. The flyer! Derrick gulped.

Joe waved the flyer in Derrick's face.

"Are you responsible for this?" he barked.

# cHapter NiNe

# PoWer Surge

Derrick swallowed hard. His mouth felt dry.

"Excuse me," a woman said, pushing between Derrick and Joe. "When can we get seated? A table of six? The name is Sweeney."

Joe glanced around the dining room. "Ah, about 30 minutes," he said. "Would you like to look at a menu while you wait?"

"Sure," the woman said as she took a menu. "This sure looks like a popular place. The food must be great.

Your flyer was right!" She smiled and walked outside.

"Now," Joe said. He waved a flyer in Derrick's face. "What is all this about? 'Follow your nose to Joe's'?"

Derrick's pulse beat in his forehead. He'd really done it now. He'd gotten himself fired—and maybe Craig too. What had he been thinking?

"I—I was just trying to help," Derrick croaked out. "I—I wanted you—us—to have more customers." He searched Joe's face for a reply.

Joe sighed. Then a smile began to creep across his face. He waved the flyers in the air. "That's what I figured," Joe said. "I guess you didn't know what a good job you could do." He swept his arm in the air. "Look at all these people. We'll be lucky to get them all waited on. I'm going to need even more help now."

Derrick looked around the restaurant. The people were busy talking. They compared notes on the menus. Some of them held his flyer in their hands. They all looked hungry.

"I'm sorry, Joe," Derrick said. He wanted to stare at the floor. But he forced himself to keep looking at Joe.

"Don't be sorry. Just get busy," Joe said. "I'll need you to serve tonight too." Then he grinned. "But none of your jokes with the customers," he warned. He elbowed Derrick. "You got them in here. Don't lose them."

Back in the kitchen, Derrick scrubbed his hands. He grabbed a red apron. Craig hustled in. He looked at Derrick.

"Not bad, little bro," Craig said grudgingly. "Guess we have enough business now. Just hope it keeps up." He stared at Derrick. "None of your comedy act now," he threatened. He grabbed three baskets of garlic bread.

"Yeah, yeah, yeah," Derrick said. Craig hurried back through the double doors with the garlic bread.

That's the best garlic *breath* in town, Derrick snickered silently. Maybe that would help the Dragon's breath. He should give her a flyer to come to Joe's. Even garlic would be better than those fumes. No, stop it! No joking around, he commanded himself. He had to get serious.

Spaghetti, lasagna, veal piccata—rush, rush, rush. Derrick wanted to crawl into bed by the end of the night. The evening had been a blur of menus, bussing dishes, carrying food in and out, and cleaning up. The last customers were just getting up from their table.

"This was great," a woman said to Joe.

"Terrific food," a man agreed. He grinned. "We'll be back. And we'll tell our friends."

"Especially about the best garlic breath in town," the woman added. She laughed.

Derrick straightened his shoulders. He puffed out his chest a little. Then he glanced around to make sure Craig hadn't seen him.

"How was work?" Mom asked when Craig and Derrick got home. "You two are home a little late," she added.

"It was so busy, you wouldn't believe it," Craig said.

"We were going crazy," Derrick chimed in.

"Joe got more customers?" Dad asked. "How?"

Derrick stopped the words from tumbling out. Would Craig tell them?

Craig glanced at Derrick. "Well, this budding comedian here . . ." He paused and pointed to Derrick. ". . . wrote up a flyer about Taste of Italy. He left it all over downtown. I guess it was kind of funny." A look of pain crossed Craig's face.

Hah! Derrick thought. Craig had to admit it! The flyer was funny! Derrick stifled a snort. He looked at Mom and Dad.

"That's great, son," Dad said with a smile. "Now all you have to do is use that same talent on your English grade. Then you'll get to keep playing football."

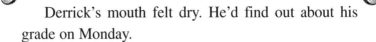

Derrick's mouth felt dry. He'd find out about his grade on Monday.

Derrick walked into English class Monday afternoon. His stomach tightened.

What's the deal? he asked himself. This wasn't any defensive back. It was only Dowling the Dragon.

Yeah, but maybe he wouldn't be facing any more defensive players if Dowling flamed his paper. His shoulders slumped a little. He sat down in his desk. Drumming his fingers, he waited for the Dragon to call roll.

"Hey!" Shaun leaned over from his desk.

"Hey, yourself," Derrick greeted back.

"Nervous about getting your paper back?" Shaun asked.

"Yeah, a little," Derrick said. He looked at the front of the room. He started to grin. "I hope there's no dragon slime on our papers when we get them," he whispered.

Shaun chuckled.

"All right, class," Mrs. Dowling said. "Enough fun." She stared right at Derrick. "I have your papers ready for you."

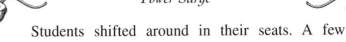

Students shifted around in their seats. A few grumbles and snickers broke out in the classroom.

Was the Dragon staring at him because he'd failed? Derrick wondered. She had no sense of humor. She probably hated his paper.

His stomach churned. He began to feel sick. It all came down to this.

Mrs. Dowling began handing papers out to students. She seemed to be moving in slow motion.

Derrick kept waiting. He thought he was going to have a heart attack. Maybe she never got his paper. Maybe she thought he never turned one in. Maybe . . .

"Derrick?" Her voice interrupted his thoughts.

Panic flooded Derrick. This was it.

"Not bad," the Dragon said. She thrust his paper at him.

*Not bad?* Derrick wanted to yell out. What did that mean?

Mrs. Dowling's eyes seemed to pop out at him. "In fact," she said, "you wrote almost like you talk. Except this time you had something important to say." She laughed her dragon laugh. The class snickered.

"Uh, thanks, Mrs. Dowling," Derrick said. He reached for his paper. What was his grade? He forced himself to look.

A big red B+ sat at the top of the page. Lots of red writing covered the margins. But he'd still gotten a B+! *Yes!* Derrick wanted to shout. He could stay in football!

"Actually, Derrick," the Dragon went on, "your grade could have been higher. If only you'd used more support for your ideas. Maybe next time," she said, walking closer to his desk. Derrick wanted to hold his nose. Her sick dragon-breath fumes were going to kill him! She *did* need Joe's garlic bread.

Mrs. Dowling finished handing out the papers. Then she moved to the front of the room.

"Let's move on," she instructed. "We're going back to the computer lab today. Get started on your creative short story assignment. Begin with a character sketch."

The class grumbled and began talking. Backpacks zipped. Binders snapped shut.

"Of course, Derrick already has a start," Mrs. Dowling said. The look on her face said she knew better. "The comedian who owns the pizza joint, right? I expect it will be quite good."

"Uh, yes, Mrs. Dowling," Derrick managed to mumble. "Not as good as the pizza though," he blurted out.

Mrs. Dowling arched her eyebrows. "Funny, Derrick," she snapped. "Let's see you write a great story. I'm sure you want to keep the football eligibility you just earned."

Derrick's head pounded. She just wasn't letting up. The class moved down the hall into the lab.

"Hope you can write another good one," Shaun

said sympathetically. He dropped into the chair next to Derrick.

Derrick shook his head. "Yeah, me too. She never quits. She must be taking extra dragon vitamins."

"Good to have the old Funny Man back," Shaun laughed. He clapped Derrick on the back.

"Get to work, guys," the Dragon barked.

All around the room, monitors were switched on. Students began typing.

Derrick took a deep breath. He sat at his same computer. Please, please, he begged silently. Let me write a good story.

He switched on the power.

Twink! The screen lit up. The word processing program loaded. Derrick waited.

The cursor blinked.

Blink! Blink! Blink!

But it wasn't typing anything.

A tiny jolt of fear flickered through Derrick. Okay, maybe he had to type something first.

**Hey, what's up? Can you help me with this character sketch? You know, my pizza comedian?** he begged in type.

His words sat alone on the screen.

Derrick peered around at the back of the computer. Nothing. He slid the mouse back and forth on the mouse pad. Still nothing.

He felt a stab of panic. He was on his own. His mouth felt dry.

Okay, Derrick thought to himself, you'll have to do this on your own. He didn't have a choice. Character sketch, huh? He took a ragged breath. Flexing his fingers, he began typing.

**Remo Hopkins. Comedian. What a guy! Everyone loves his comedy routines. Makes jokes to get out of sticky situations . . .**

His fingers moved faster and faster. He hardly noticed the time draining away. He jumped when the bell rang.

"You're dismissed, class," Mrs. Dowling announced. "Save your work, and print it out."

Derrick saved his sketch on his disk. He printed out the page he'd written. Then he leaned over to Shaun.

He grinned. "Hey, listen to my character." He began reading his page aloud.

"Cool!" Shaun said after Derrick finished. He laughed. "I like the spaghetti twister."

Derrick stood up. He reached behind the computer to turn it off.

He never saw the cursor on the screen blinking at him.

**See?   I   said   you   could   do   this   by   yourself!** the computer typed.

Twink! The screen went dark.

But Derrick was already walking down the aisle.

"Let's go," he said to Shaun and Rod. "We have a game to win." He grinned. "And *that's* no joke."